47 Beavers
ON THE BIG, BLUE SEA

By
Phil Vischer

Illustrated by Jared Chapman

Characters Designed by Dana Thompson

Tommy NELSON

A Division of Thomas Nelson Publishers

NASHVILLE   DALLAS   MEXICO CITY   RIO DE JANEIRO

FORTY-SEVEN BEAVERS ON THE BIG, BLUE SEA
Copyright © 2006 by Phil Vischer.
Illustrator: Jared Chapman
Character designs: Dana Thompson
Design by Portland Studios.

Thomas Nelson, Inc., titles may be purchased in bulk for educational, business, fundraising,
or sales promotional use. For information, please email SpecialMarkets@ThomasNelson.com.

Library of Congress Cataloging-in-Publication Data
Vischer, Phil.
Forty-seven beavers on the big, blue sea / written by Phil Vischer; illustrated by Jared
Chapman ; character designs by Dana Thompson.
  p. cm.
Summary: In 1842, forty-seven beavers escape from the man who trapped them
and row out into the Pacific Ocean, where they encounter terrible dangers and begin to
despair until they realize that by using their God-given strengths and working together,
they can reach safety.
ISBN-13: 978-1-4003-0836-1 (hardcover)
ISBN-13: 978-1-4003-1184-2 (softcover)
[1. Beavers—Fiction. 2. Cooperativeness—Fiction. 3. Pacific Northwest—History—
19th century—Fiction. 4. Stories in rhyme.] I. Chapman, Jared, ill. II. Thompson,
Dana. III. Title.
PZ8.3.V74For 2007
[E]—dc22   2006011450

Printed in China.
12 13 14 RRD 6 5 4 3 2

"Two are better than one,
because they have a good reward
for their toil.
For if they fall, one will lift up the other."
—*Ecclesiastes 4:9,10*

"Forty-seven are even better than two."

—*Phil*

Deep in the northwest territ'ry,
Where the woods look down
    on the western sea
And the trappers trap so merrily
For the streams are oh so beaver-y,

One day, in 1842,
A trapper by the name of Stu
Came down to the beach and said, "Halloo!
I need a boat, or a big canoe!"

"I need a lift on down the coast
To the nearest beaver trading post

Where they'll shake my hand and raise a toast
To Trapper Stu, who trapped the most!"

So he piled what he caught in a rather small boat
And asked the young sailor to give him a quote.
"No way!" said the sailor, with fear in his throat.
"There's too many beavers! It ain't gonna float!"

And as they debated, man to man,
The beavers developed a curious plan . . .

And the beavers pulled upon the oars
And the beavers rowed away from shore
And the beavers two, and the beavers three,
Forty-seven beavers on the big, blue sea!

No one thought that beavers were capable of scheming.
If you'd say, "They'll row away," most folks would say
    you're dreaming.
But here they were and there they went across the
    briny blue,
Calling out a cadence like a real Olympic crew!

For a week or two the beaver crew rowed the great Pacific,
Till from the north a storm blew in with winds that were terrific!
And one by one, their oars blew off and vanished! Mercy me!
And forty-seven beavers were left bobbin' in the sea!

Well the beavers bobbed upon the sea
And the beavers sobbed in misery
And the beavers two, and the beavers three,
Forty-seven beavers on the big, blue sea!

"This is bad!" they cried. "We feel like
    Noah in his ark!"
Then their bad got worse, cuz they were
    starin' at a shark!

"Alas, alack, we're doomed!" they wailed.
The shark showed his incisors.
"Adrift at sea, and now we'll be
a fishy's appetizers!"

Then one small beaver stood and faced the others from the bow.
He said, "Our time will come someday, but it ain't comin' now.
When we all work together, there's a lot that we can do!
So let's show that big bully that we've got incisors, too!"

Ninety-four big beaver teeth flashed out from the boat.
One old shark was so surprised his heart jumped in his throat.
"Never mind," he muttered as he vanished in the blue.
"It's no fun bitin' dinner if your dinner's bitin' you."

Well the beavers flashed their pearly whites
And the shark he vanished out of sight
And the beavers two, and the beavers three,
Forty-seven beavers on the big, blue sea!

"That's good," they said. "But we're still stuck!
    We'll die here on a reef!"
"Not so fast!" the young one said.
    "God gave us more than teeth!"

With that he jumped back to the stern, and
      dangled down his tail,
And started slappin' water like a little beaver whale!

Soon the others joined him, and with all that
    beaver power,
Their little boat was skimmin' waves at
    forty miles an hour!

And the beavers slapped their big, flat tails
And the beavers raced like killer whales
And the beavers two, and the beavers three,
Forty-seven beavers on the big, blue sea!

Three more weeks went by, and soon they all began to mope.
"We're gettin' tired of paddlin'. We're startin' to lose hope!"
Then ahead they saw a sight that made them holler, "Wowie!"
Forty-seven beavers—had just discovered Maui.

They hit the land and kissed the sand—
a sign of their thanksgiving.
But soon began to mope again,
"How will we make a living?"

"This island ain't for beavers, and we're
not pedicurists."
"I've got it!" cried the little guy.
"We'll entertain the tourists!"

So the beavers built a beaver lodge
And the tourists came for food and fudge
And the beavers two—what do you know!
Forty-seven beavers in a dinner show!

So why'd I tell this story? What's the point for me and you?
We might find ourselves someday trapped by Trapper Stu,
Or staring down our own big sharks or facing nasty weather,
But we've been blessed, and things go best when we all
      work together!

And the beavers pulled upon the oars
And the beavers rowed away from shore
And the beavers two, and the beavers three,
Forty-seven beavers on the big, blue sea!